Andy Pandy
and the hedgehog

Story by Maria Bird, illustrated by Matvyn Wright

BROCKHAMPTON PRESS, LEICESTER

AND THE POTATO PRESS, CHICAGO

Published in 1973 in the United States of America by J. Philip O'Hara Inc,
Chicago and in Great Britain by Brockhampton Press Limited, Leicester
Published simultaneously in Canada by Van Nostrand Reinhold Limited, Scarborough, Ontario
This edition Copyright © Andy Pandy Limited 1973
Printed in Great Britain by Purnell and Sons Limited

One day Andy Pandy and Teddy
were playing on a little hill in the
garden, when they saw something moving
slowly through the grass. They ran to
see what it was. "Look Teddy," said
Andy, "it's a prickly hedgehog."

"Is it called a prickly ickly hedgehog
because it's got prickles all over?"
asked Teddy, and he put his little fat
paw out to stroke the hedgehog.
But the hedgehog rolled itself up into
a round prickly ickly ball.

"Oh dear," said Teddy, "it has
rolled its face up inside itself."
"Never mind, Teddy," said
Andy Pandy. "I know how to make
him unroll," and he ran indoors
and poured out a saucer of milk.

Andy Pandy carried the saucer of milk
back very carefully and put it down
close to the prickly ickly hedgehog.
When it smelt the milk, it uncurled
itself, poked out its little face,
and began to drink.

Teddy was so pleased that he began
jumping about, and when all the milk
had gone, he picked up the saucer, and,
by mistake, touched the hedgehog, which
turned itself into a ball again, and
began to roll away down the hill.

"Oh, Andy," said Teddy. "I wish we could make
ourselves round and roll down the hill too."
"Let's try," said Andy Pandy.
He could curl up, but Teddy
couldn't make himself roll
because he was so square behind.

"Perhaps if I looked more like the
hedgehog, I could roll better,"
he thought. And he went off by
himself while Andy Pandy sat
down at the bottom of the hill with
the prickly ickly hedgehog.

"What I need is prickles all over,"
said Teddy to himself. "What can I make
them with? I know—*clothes pegs!*
I'll go off to find some. Not
nearly enough," he thought,
so he went to find Andy Pandy.

"I want more pegs," he said.
"Whatever for?" said Andy Pandy.
"I want to do something special," said Teddy.
"Well," said Andy Pandy, "there
are lots more in the kitchen."
So Teddy trotted off to get them.

Then Andy Pandy went back to the
house to get some more milk for the
hedgehog. He wondered what Teddy
was up to. He didn't think Teddy
could be washing his clothes because
he only wore a bow.

He soon found out when he saw
Teddy coming down the path
all covered with clothes pegs.
"Whatever are you doing?"
he cried. "You don't look
like my teddy at all."

"I'm not," said Teddy. "I'm a prickly ickly hedgehog. You watch." And he curled himself up and tried to roll down the hill just like the hedgehog. But he still couldn't curl himself into a ball. Andy laughed so much he spilt some of the milk.

The pretty little animal drank up the spilt
milk and another saucerful as well, taking
tiny little sips with its little pink tongue.
Then Teddy, who still believed he looked
just like a hedgehog, sat down on the
ground and started to drink too.

"Now," said Andy Pandy, "I'm going to take off all your clothes pegs and put them away, because I really like you best without. Bears are bears, and prickly ickly hedgehogs are prickly ickly hedgehogs."

So they went into the house, and it took Andy
a long time to get all the clothes pegs off.
Then they sat down by the fire and the little
hedgehog sat between them. And they were all
very happy to be just what they were, a little
boy, a little bear, and a prickly ickly hedgehog.